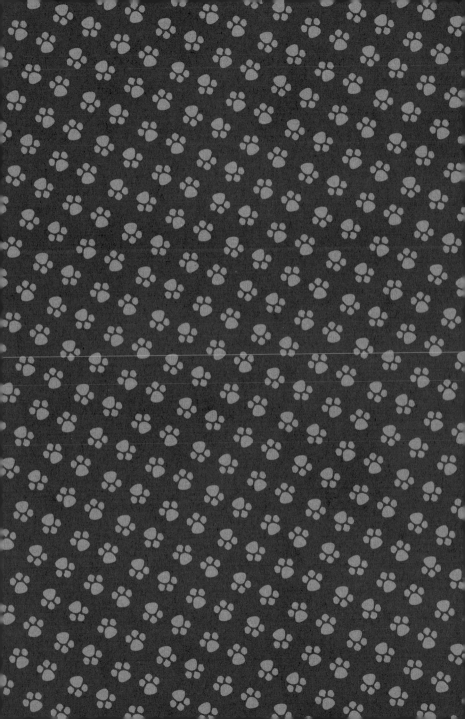

HELPER HOUNDS

Brisket

Helps Miryam with Online Learning

Dedication
To the Fine Folks at Chicago Animal Care and Control.
You rescued two of my dogs from the streets. I am forever grateful.

HELPER HOUNDS

Brisket

Helps Miryam with Online Learning

Caryn Dahlstrand Rivadeneira

Caryn Rivadeneira
Illustrated by Priscilla Alpaugh

RED CHAIR ·PRESS·

Egremont, Massachusetts

Red Chair Press
BOOKS FOR YOUNG READERS

www.redchairpress.com

 Free educator's guide at www.redchairpress.com/free-resources

Publisher's Cataloging-In-Publication Data

Names: Rivadeneira, Caryn Dahlstrand, author. | Alpaugh, Priscilla, illustrator. | Rivadeneira, Caryn Dahlstrand. Helper hounds.

Title: Brisket helps Miryam with online learning / Caryn Rivadeneira; illustrated by Priscilla Alpaugh.

Description: Egremont, Massachusetts: Red Chair Press, [2021] | Series: Helper Hounds | Includes fun facts and information about the dog breed, Lakeland Terrier. | Summary: "Miryam's body doesn't fight off germs like it should. While doctors figure out how to make her better, Miryam needs to stay home for online classes. Trouble is: Miryam struggles to focus on her teacher and schoolwork ... When Miryam's dad hears about the Helper Hounds, everything changes. Brisket the Helper Hound knows all about learning to focus and about staying in touch with friends"-- Provided by publisher.

Identifiers: ISBN 9781643710808 (hardcover) | ISBN 9781643710815 (paperback) | ISBN 9781643710822 (ebook)

Subjects: LCSH: Lakeland terrier--Juvenile fiction. | Attention in children--Juvenile fiction. | Sick children--Juvenile fiction. | Distance education--Juvenile fiction. | CYAC: Terriers--Fiction. | Attention--Fiction. | Sick children--Fiction. | Distance education--Fiction.

Classification: LCC PZ7.1.R57627 Br 2021 (print) | LCC PZ7.1.R57627 (ebook) | DDC [E]--dc23

Library of Congress Control Number: 2020948973

Photos: iStock

Printed in the United States of America

0421 1P CGF21

CHAPTER 1

Well, hellooooooooooo!

I lifted my shaggy snout into the air and barked.

Zahra, the girl on the other side of the screen, smiled and waved back with a wide-open hand.

"Whatcha, Brisket!" Zahra said. "It's been forever since we talked."

"Well, hello to you too," Luke said, with a laugh.

Luke is my guy. He saved my life once. Then, he helped me become a World-Famous Helper Hound.

"Oh, sorry, Mr. Luke," Zahra said. "It's just so nice to see Brisket off of social media! You've been on lots of good bimbles there in America, haven't you?"

I put my front paws on the desk and panted. I missed London a lot—especially living near Zahra. But I did get to take lots of good walks—or *bimbles*, as we used to call them—here in our new city. We had so many great smells. I loved taking them all in.

"So, what's new?" Luke asked. "How's life?

"Well," Zahra said. "I've been dying to tell you. Rufus got a *dog*. Can you believe that? And it looks just like you—except *huge*. It's an Airedale Terrier. They rescued it from the same place where Luke adopted you—the R.S.P...?"

"...C.A.?" Luke said.

"That's right," Zahra said. "But guess what they named it?"

Luke and I were silent. I sat down straight.

My tail swished across Luke's lap.

"Guess!" Zahra said again.

"Brisket?" Luke said finally.

"No! They aren't that big of copycats!" Zahra said. "But it *is* a food. Alright. I'll just tell you: Kale Salad. Can you believe that? A dog named after the grossest food of all time?"

"Brilliant! I love kale salad," Luke said.

Zahra shook her head. "My mom likes it too. But it's not a good name for a dog. Kale salad is green and healthy. This dog is always muddy and naughty! He gets into so much trouble. I'm trying to help Rufus work with him. But Kale Salad won't focus. He's all over the place. Kale Salad just wants to run wild!"

"Well," said Luke. "That sounds familiar!"

Luke smiled and clucked his tongue. I reached up to kiss him.

"Do you remember how Brisket used to be?" Luke asked. "When I first rescued him?"

"Not really," Zahra said. "I was little then."

"Well, we had to work a lot on how to focus," Luke said. "Brisket was a wild, wild terrier. Just like Kale Salad. Here, let me show you something to help."

Luke slid his computer monitor back. He called me up on the desk and stood up so Zahra could get a better look.

My tail slid like a rudder across the desk. Two pens and a notebook fell to the floor with a tap and a thunk.

"Careful with that tail," Zahra laughed.

But my eyes were no longer on the screen. My eyes were on the liver treat in his hands. Luke brought it to his eyes and said, "Focus!" in his chirpy "dog voice." My eyes locked on his. My tail stood stick straight. I didn't move an inch. Luke flipped me the liver treat.

"Good boy, Brisket," Luke said. "See how easy that is? I bet you could teach this to Kale Salad. Just grab a treat, bring it to your nose, and say, "Focus!" When Kale Salad makes eye contact, give him the treat and praise like crazy. You can train Rufus to do the same."

Luke smiled. Zahra giggled.

"Rufus McGuiken better never look me in the eyes," she said. "I'd give him a treat all right."

Luke laughed out loud and sat me back on his lap. He scratched my head while I thought about Rufus.

I thought Rufus was tops. But Zahra and Rufus never got along. They fought over me, mostly. Over who could walk me, to be precise.

Most days, Zahra would knock on the door and offer to take me for a walk while Luke worked. Most days, Luke said yes, tossed Zahra my leash, and off we'd go.

As soon as we left, Rufus would bound out of his door and insist that he come with us. This drove Zahra crazy.

Zahra was nine months older than Rufus. And those nine months gave Zahra the "right" to be trusted to take a wild Brisket like me to the park and make sure I ran through my obedience drills. Since Rufus was "way younger," his job was to make sure I got all my zoomies in and wiggles out.

If you ask me, the two of them made the perfect combination for an afternoon at the park. Even if they both bickered a lot.

"Zahra," Luke said. "I'm sorry. But we'll have to video-chat another time. Just got an alert that we've got a new case."

Luke scratched my wiry fur and asked if I was ready for a new job. I barked, YES!

"I better let you go straightaway then," Zahra said. "Anyway, Mom just got home. Dad has tea ready, and Mom will want to know how my homework is coming along."

Luke smiled. "Hope we haven't kept you from it."

"Not at all! I learned something new. I'll tell Rufus about it after tea. Goodbye, Brisket!"

"He says goodbye," Luke said.

I panted at the screen as Luke waved.

Zahra's face blinked off the screen, and the Helper Hounds logo flashed on. While Luke read about our new case, I jumped off his lap to scratch an itch deep in my left ear.

"Well, how's this case sound, Briskie? Remember when Zahra and Rufus had to go to school online during the pandemic? Well, Miryam's doctor says she should do her classes online this semester. She doesn't like it. Miryam is having a hard time paying attention. That's *just* what we were talking about!"

Or, I think that's what he said. My nail was scratching deep inside my floppy ear.

No bother. No matter what he said, I knew I could help Miryam. I was brilliant at helping people—thanks to the people who helped me when I needed it most.

CHAPTER 2

I told you earlier that I'm the sort of terrier who needs to get his zoomies out. Have I told you I'm a Lakeland Terrier, to be exact? Anyway, Lakelands—or "Lakies"—are short and squat and curly. Below my tan hair and black "saddle" lies nothing but muscle and energy, bounce and pounce. I'm always ready to go.

This is a *good* thing when Zahra or Rufus come to get me for a walk. And it's a good thing when we get a new Helper Hounds case. I'm up for anything! But my boundless energy has gotten me into trouble a time or two. One time, most of all.

I was six months old, and my name wasn't even Brisket yet! The people I lived with chose me from a batch of high-energy Lakies bred by a farmer down the road. They didn't give me much thought. I was just so cute, so curly, so friendly, that they couldn't pass me up. So, my first family slid a bunch of twenty-pound notes into the farmer's hand and plopped me into his wife's bicycle basket. The girl said my name should be Tiger, because I looked like one. (I don't!) They all agreed and then the whole family cycled off down a long path. When we got to their farm, they parked their bikes and created a space for me in their barn.

I loved it. I slept on piles of soft hay and old clothes. I ate when the other animals ate (an old pony, three sheep, and a crabby barn cat). And I got to follow my fancy. I explored every corner of that old barn. I sniffed around old milk pails and behind creaky ladders. I climbed on hay

bales and peed on old feed buckets. Then one
day, I discovered a secret—a secret exit, that is.
Some mice had chewed through a loose board
in the pony's stall. This offered the perfect
amount of space for me to squeeze through.
And boy, did I squeeze through!

Every day, I'd slink my body through the slot
and let my nose lead me through the beautiful
English countryside. If my nose smelled a fox,

I'd follow the fox scent to the left. If my nose smelled a cow in the meadow, I'd turn to find the cows. If my nose smelled Mr. Hammer's fresh sausages frying away in town, I'd zoom over the hills and wander through the winding lanes until I found Mr. Hammer's sausage shop. It was the best life.

My people weren't fond of my wanderings. They got tired of the local constable, that's an English police officer, bringing me back home with a warning. The constable would tell them to tie me up—or teach me some obedience. But they'd just pop me back in the barn and soon enough, I'd wander off again. And another constable would bring me back home.

Until one day, the constable turned the wrong way down the road to the farm.

"Time for your people to learn a lesson," he said. "You're a good little fellow. But your people don't seem to know how to mind you. Maybe they'll learn to look after you once they've had to shell out a few quid to get you back!"

And so, the constable dropped me off at our local RSPCA. At least, that's what he called it. I learned later it was the *Royal* Society for the Prevention of Cruelty to Animals. Sounds both fancy *and* scary, but it was very casual and comfy!

The nice people there gathered me up. They combed my hair for lice and ticks (I had a few). And then set me in a small kennel with a cozy bed and some fresh water and food.

The constable stopped by my kennel to say goodbye.

"Hope I don't see you again, little buddy," he said. "Hope your owners do better by you." Then he snuck a treat through the gate. I took it gently, and he turned to leave.

I barked and barked after he left. I wasn't even sure why. It wasn't like I knew him—or

even liked him. It just suddenly felt very, very lonely in the back, away from the sounds and smells of the barn or the outside world.

I hopped on my kennel gates. I pushed my snout all around. Surely there must be a way out! But there wasn't. So I sat and barked and barked and whined and whined.

Soon one of the nice ladies who had combed for fleas came to check on me.

"Time for us to leave, love," she said as she knelt in front of my cage. "We rung your people. No one answered. I'll be back in the morning. We'll ring them again then."

She slipped her fingers through the cage and rubbed my nose.

"You be a good boy," she said. "Snuggle down and get some rest. You've had a big day. We're having brisket for dinner tonight. If you're good, I'll sneak you a piece of leftovers in the morning."

She made a kissy sound toward me. I stood to kiss her back. Then she stood up and walked away. I heard a click and the Royal Society for the Prevention of Cruelty to Animals got very, very dark.

CHAPTER 3

Somehow, I slept. I slept through the barking of dogs all around me. I slept through the hiss of cats in the next room. I slept through the rumble of thunder to the east. If sleeping in a barn taught me anything, it was how to sleep anywhere.

I woke up to a smell of smoked meat. I cracked my eyes open and saw the source right away.

The lady was back!

"Look what I brought you," she said and slipped a bit of meat through the cage. "It's some leftover brisket!"

She snapped
the clip on a
bright red leash
and asked if I'd
like a walk through
their back garden.

I stood up, and my
tail buzzed into action.
Of course, I would!

As we walked down a pebble path,
I tugged at the leash and raced ahead. I wasn't
used to being held back! But the lady tried her
best to keep up as I sniffed around new trees
and bushes that smelled of old dog wee. The
lady told me about the phone call with my
people.

"Well, good news and bad, Tiger," she said.

I looked up at the sound of my name—even
though I wasn't very used to it.

Then she shook her head. "Tiger isn't even

a good name for you, love," she said. "You're nothing like a Tiger—aside from the colors. No, I'd say you're more like a... a... Brisket?"

I stopped and wagged my tail. She said it again, "Brisket."

Something about the way she said it—chirped it really—just made me feel really great. *Loved it*, I'd learn to call that feeling later.

"Yes, Brisket. That's better." We walked on and the lady kept talking. "So, bad news is that your people decided you run away too much. They don't want you back. 'Too much trouble,' they said."

She shook her head and knelt to scratch my ears.

I put my front feet on her lap.

"Shame," she said. "You're a good little dog. But the good news is somebody else will notice that. You're gonna find someone to love you as you should be loved."

Just then something rustled in the bushes. I shot off her lap to look. Poor lady tumbled back onto her, well, backside.

She laughed and she scrambled to catch me. "But that person is gonna have to love you enough to train you and teach you that you can't just follow your nose everywhere."

• • •

Four days later, that person showed up.

Luke was early for a meeting in town so he wandered over to the RSPCA. I heard his funny accent (*American*, I'd later learn) and loud laugh all the way down the hall. The voice grew louder and louder as the lady walked him toward my kennel.

"I know you said you don't have much space in your flat, but London's got such lovely parks...," the lady was saying. "If you could just work with this fellow, teach him some tricks and what not, make sure he gets his walks in, he'd be a great little companion for you."

The man—Luke—knelt in front of my cage.

"I hear you like to run away," Luke said. "That could be a problem. I just had my heart broken. I can't have anybody else running away on me!"

The lady giggled.

"I can't imagine anyone running away on *you*," she said. The man raised an eyebrow. I pawed at the cage.

There was something I liked about this man. Maybe it was his fresh smell. Maybe it was his big voice. Maybe it was the way his eyes sparkled when he looked at me.

One quick walk and a short visit to the "adoption office" later and my life changed completely. The lady walked me over to the vet's surgery for a "quick snip," as she called it. Then two days later, she drove me to London to visit Luke again. She ooh-ed and ahh-ed about his flat with big windows and a sunny terrace. She looked over the bags of food and the toys and bed Luke had bought. Finally, she nodded.

"Well done," she said. Then the lady handed Luke a brochure. "I'd get him in obedience classes right away. It will help his focus and that terrier 'selective deafness' Brisket has got. Of course, you don't have to call him Brisket…"

"I already signed *Brisket* up for obedience training," Luke said. "He and I need something to keep our minds off the heartbreaks of our past."

"Well, good luck to you, then!" the lady said. "I hope the future is full of joy and *love* for you both!"

She thanked Luke for adopting me and said she would be happy to help any time in the future. Perhaps even over dinner?

Luke laughed and said, "Maybe."

I'd soon learn that ladies often wanted to have dinner with Luke. There was something they seemed to like about him, too.

But for now, Luke was mine. All mine. And he and I were about to start an amazing adventure neither of us saw coming.

CHAPTER 4

Let me cut to the chase. Obviously, Luke and I
loved each other right away. I loved his flat and
made friends very quickly—as I already told
you.

The only trouble was that I liked to, well,
cut to the chase. I had a bit of a focus
problem. I'd notice a fly or an
ant or a piece of bread and
then I'd race around his
apartment, run over the
furniture, zip across
counters. You name it: if
it caught my eye or the

scent caught my nose, I'd zoom to check it out!

It took Luke about two days to realize I needed to learn to focus and learn some manners. He took me to the obedience class at the park straightaway. Then, something amazing happened. Turns out, I'm great at obedience. After the walk to the park and some time zooming around with Luke chasing squirrels, I could pay attention better than any of the other dogs.

In fact, I got *so* good at obedience, I began to win competitions! Imagine that! Then, Luke set me up with social media, and things got really crazy. Not only was I a champion at obedience trials, I was *famous*. Social-media famous. Hundreds of thousands of people followed and liked posts—of me sleeping, me going on bimbles with Luke or Zahra and Rufus, of me doing a perfect stand-stay, of me swimming, of me sailing, of me eating pizza... You get the

idea. People stopped me in the park or on the
sidewalks—sometimes even when I was "using
the loo," as we say. They wanted pictures with
me to post on their own social media.

So, when a man walked up to Luke after one
obedience competition, I sat nicely. I thought
he wanted my picture. He *did* want my picture,

but this man also wanted something else. He had noticed how nice and calm I was around all the folks who took pictures with me. He was impressed by one video that showed me snuggling Zahra after she tripped and skinned her knee. (Rufus took the video while we waited for Luke to come help.)

The man handed Luke a card and said, "My name's Tuttle. I run a program called Helper

Hounds. If you're ever in America…"

Luke shook his hand and said, "Well, that might be sooner than you think."

And it was! Two weeks later, boxes filled our flat. Zahra sat next to me crying and crying. I leaned in close. Rufus stood tall and tight and tried not to cry. I licked his face all over when he knelt to say goodbye.

They stood outside and waved for a long time as the car drove us to Heathrow Airport. I woofed my goodbye: to my friends and to England. We were going to America!

• • •

Luke was already from America. He knew that people talked funny (like him!) and that they drove on the *wrong* side of the road. Luke knew all the things that were different. But they were all new to me. As different as America was from England, we still lived in a flat (though now we called it an *apartment*). The people were still nice. The food was still good. The parks were still green. I was still great at obedience. And I was still really famous on social media. Plus, there was one more thing.

I became an official Helper Hound! We didn't even know about them in England. But Mr. Tuttle invited us to Helper Hounds University. We went a few months after we arrived, and guess what? I passed with flying colors. I joined an amazing team of dogs and got to do the coolest things. I mean, I *get* to do the coolest things.

Like now: We're walking to the train so we can meet Miryam. Just three stops and one transfer until we can help her focus on her online classes.

CHAPTER 5

A screen door flew open and a little girl came running out. She adjusted her mask as she stopped at the end of the sidewalk.

"Must be Miryam," Luke said.

He told me to sit and then leaned down to tidy me up. We had walked three blocks from the train station. The wind blew my beard all wonky and twisted my Helper Hounds vest around my waist. Luke reached into his pocket and put his mask on.

"Is that Brisket?" Miryam yelled.

"It is," Luke said.

Miryam turned and ran back to the house.

"*Daaaaaaaaad!*" she yelled.

We stopped at the end of a walkway to Miryam's house. A man opened the screen door and waved us inside. I trotted nicely up the walkway next to Luke.

"You must be Dad," Luke said. He was smiling behind his mask. I could tell.

"I am indeed," the man said. His eyebrows arched above his mask. "I'm Malik."

Malik held out a fist. Luke did the same. They moved their fists into the air but never bumped. I didn't have to worry about germs, so I sat in front of the man. He petted me until Miryam came running down the stairs.

"Easy, Mir," Malik said. "I know you're excited, but you're going to scare Brisket."

"Brisket's not easily scared," Luke said. "But your dad is right: most dogs don't like people running up to them!"

"I'm sorry," Miryam said. "I'm just soooooooooo excited. And when I'm excited, I need to get my wiggles out! Plus, I wanted to show Brisket this. I drew it!"

Miryam held up a drawing of a fuzzy dog with brown fur and a black saddle. It looked like me!

"Wow!" Luke said. "That's terrific. That

looks like Brisket, and you sound a lot like Brisket. He needs to get his wiggles out too. That's the only way he can concentrate enough to win those obedience medals."

"He's won *medals*?" Miryam asked.

"Sure has," Luke said. "I can show you some pictures."

Miryam's eyes widened. "Can I pet him first?"

"Of course," Luke said. "I forgot you weren't here for introductions. Let him sniff your hand and then scratch him—right on the black part."

Luke told me to stand. But he didn't really need to tell me. I knew the drill.

I stood and sniffed Miryam's hand. I smelled small amounts of sweat covered by the sharp aroma of hand sanitizer. I licked her quick before she moved her hand toward my back. Miryam was great at scratching.

"How about we sit down," Malik said as he

motioned toward the kitchen down the hall.
"Since you lived in London so long, I made us
some tea—and I have both dog *and* human
biscuits."

Luke laughed. "Wonderful," Luke said. He
handed Miryam my leash. "Can you walk
Brisket into the kitchen? You should get used

to him so you can walk him in case we want to head to the park later."

Miryam raised her eyebrows high above her mask and picked up my leash. Together we ran to the kitchen. I beat her by a full terrier length.

"He's little, but he's fast!" Miryam said.

Miryam, Malik, and Luke pulled out chairs and sat. I lay down on the floor next to everyone. Malik poured tea for the humans. He put down a bowl of water for me. I slurped and slurped as Luke kept talking.

"He is fast," Luke said. "You should've seen him when I first brought him home! Little guy would fly around our flat—I mean, *apartment*—

like he had wings. Any little motion—a fly, a mouse, a shadow—would set him off. He was always zooming. This was fine when I had time to play. But when I had to work, I needed Brisket to settle down. This is why we got into obedience classes—and then competitions."

"So that's why Brisket is here? He can help me settle down and pay attention?" Miryam said.

Luke laughed. "Well, Brisket can show you what he does—and then we can see if it works for you too."

Miryam nodded slowly. "That makes sense," she said. "I wondered how a dog was going to teach me."

"Well, this dog teaches me something every day," Luke said. "Your dad said you guys have a garden out back. How about we head out there and you can tell me more about online learning and Brisket can show you some of his tricks."

Miryam scooted back hard on her chair before anyone could answer. I don't scare easily, but I'll admit: the sound of the *screeeeetch* across the floor made me jump.

"May I?" Luke asked as he snatched the dog biscuits off the table. "These always help Brisket focus."

Malik nodded, and Miryam snatched a human biscuit for herself.

CHAPTER 6

Miryam let go of my leash as soon as we stepped off the back deck into the cool green grass.

"Is it okay if he runs around?" she asked. "Can I show him our play-set?"

"How about we save the play-set for later," Luke said. "But yes, it's always good for him to get his zoomies out. Run him around! Then I want to hear about what's going on with school."

Malik nodded toward Miryam. "Take Brisket on a good zoom around the yard."

And off we went. I outran Miryam, of

course, but not by much. I ran right to her play-set. I thought of Zahra and Rufus at the park. They loved this kind of stuff. I did too! But with my Helper Hounds vest on, I wasn't supposed to be playing on slides. So I managed to take in two quick sniffs of the slide without trying to climb up it. *Maybe later*, I thought.

When we got back to the deck, Miryam stopped. I kept running until Luke called me back. Then Miryam and I sat on a long wooden bench.

"So," Luke said. "Your dad told us some of the e-learning issues in the email. But how about you tell us how Brisket can help?"

"Well, I can't go back to school right now because of my *immune system*. It's compromised, which means I catch too many colds and viruses. I have to do *all* my classes online. Which stinks! I miss being in school and playing with my friends. And I don't feel like I can focus long enough to learn anything! Can Brisket help? Maybe he can sit with me all day at school?"

Luke laughed. "He probably can't sit with you all day, but he can show you a few of his tricks—things that have helped him focus."

"Like obedience tricks?" Miryam said.

"Yes, actually," Luke said. "Watch."

Luke clucked his tongue and told me to
stand. Then he told me to stay and crossed the
yard. Luke danced and flapped his arms and
turned windmills. I didn't move a muscle. I
stayed perfectly still in my stand-stay. A bird
flew above me. A cricket chirped in the yard
ahead. A squirrel skitted across the top of their
fence. I stood like a statue.

Then Luke said, "Turkey!"

Then, "Lemon."

Then, "Kumquat."

I didn't move. I kept my eyes firmly on Luke's face and my ears perfectly tuned to hear the words I waited for.

"Come!" Luke said suddenly. I bolted forward and sat right in front of Luke.

He told me I was a good boy and released me to play with a loud, "Okay!"

Luke and I trotted back across the yard.

Luke said, "When I first brought Brisket home, I couldn't even get him to look up at me for more than a second. He was too busy following the whole world around him. There was just so much that he was worried about missing out on..."

"FOMO! Fear of Missing Out! That's what I have," said Miryam.

"Yes," Luke said. "I get it too. I think we all

do. It's hard to focus on one thing because we don't want to miss all the *other* things. Brisket? Are you even paying attention?"

I snapped my head toward Luke. I'll admit: The breeze blowing through the bushes had caught my eye. And then I just *had* to watch the squirrel tip-toe across a tree branch. But being a Helper Hound means when I've got my vest on, I always keep one ear tuned to hear my name!

"Good boy," Luke said. "See? Brisket *still* has trouble focusing. But that's okay. Because we know the tricks to get him back—and I think those tricks can help you too."

Miryam smiled. "I bet I already know one of the tricks," she said.

"Oh yeah?" Luke asked.

"Yeah, getting our *zooooooomies* out!" she said.

"That's right!" Luke said. "And if you want to race him back to the deck, we can talk about the rest when we get there. Ready, set, go!"

At that, Miryam took off running. Luke released me and I ran after her.

"I *almost won*," Miryam said as she slumped into her chair.

Her dad laughed. "Yes, almost, sweetie…"

Malik refilled their water glasses and my bowl and then offered another round of biscuits. I chomped mine down and lay nicely at Miryam's feet.

CHAPTER 7

Luke told everyone more about the history of Helper Hounds and how I was the first *international* hound. Then Luke told his favorite dog-dad joke: "Brisket picked up the language here pretty well though…"

Everyone always laughed at this joke. But for Luke, this was usually the beginning of a lecture!

"Here's what's weird about dogs," Luke began. "Dogs *do* understand actual human words—in whatever language they're taught. But dogs rely on the way you smell or the way you look far more than the sound you make to understand what's going on. That's actually one of Brisket's tips for helping *me* focus."

Miryam scrunched her eyebrows.

"Like that!" Luke said. "I know you're confused because of the way you moved your face. If I pay attention to more than just *what* you say, but *how* you say it or how you look, I'm better focused!"

Miryam nodded. "My gramma does that," she said. "*Miryam, you look worried...* She always says when we're online!"

"Your grandmother used to tell *me* I 'looked worried' even before we had camera phones!" Malik said.

Luke laughed. "My mother tells me she can 'hear it in my voice.' It sounds funny, but body language or tone of voice says so much. We're not so different from dogs—we use this for communicating too! And one of the best parts of online school is that you get a great chance to notice your teacher's body language and listen to tones without all the distractions of a classroom."

"But I've got the distractions of my room!" Miryam said.

"Well, that's another suggestion," Luke said. "When Brisket began his training, we took a long walk to get *all* his wiggles out. Then, when we got back to the flat. I closed the windows and put his toys away. That helped him focus on me. Then, when we started practicing obedience, we'd set a timer—starting at five minutes, then ten, and so on. I knew Brisket was in the 'zone' when his tongue hung out. Not only was he happy, but he was taking good breaths, which helps too! And all throughout training, I'd reward him with praise and great treats. Knowing we have a reward really helps us focus."

"So, having my phone and my gaming console next to me might not be helping me focus?" Miryam said.

"Probably not," Malik said. "But I could make your favorite banana bars as rewards!"

"Brisket prefers liver sausage to banana bars, but I bet those would help!" Luke said.

Miryam pretended to gag and shook her head at Brisket.

"How can you eat that?" she said. Miryam reached down to scratch my ear.

"Remember, he was a *stray* for a while. I bet he ate a lot worse than that when he had to sort through the garbage."

It had been a long time since I'd eaten out of the garbage. But Luke always made it sound bad. But really, I had some great meals that way! I was about to daydream about my best food-trash finds, when Miryam made a sudden announcement.

"All this talk about *focus* got me in the mood for the *best* tip," Miryam said. "We should get our wiggles out again. Can I take him for a spin around the yard?"

Luke told her to go for it. Miryam grabbed my leash and took off running. That's when tragedy struck.

I had followed Miryam right up the rope ladder on the play-set.

"I can't believe he can climb this thing!"
Miryam yelled down. "He's like a circus dog!
Will he go down the slide?"

"He will!" Luke said. "But wait. Let me take
off his vest…"

Luke had begun running across the yard. But it was too late. I knew better than to play with my Helper Hounds vest on, but Miryam tugged my leash and pulled me down the slide. At least, she pulled me until my vest caught on a screw and I got stuck *in* the slide. Had I mentioned this was a *tube* slide?

Miryam tugged and tugged, but I didn't budge. I barked twice inside the tube and hoped Luke would scramble up to save me. But the tube was narrow and Luke is *wide*. He played American football in college. There was no way he could come and save me. It was true that I wasn't afraid of much, but being stuck in this tube scared me. I whined and whined.

Luke's head popped down the top of the tube. "It's okay, buddy," he said. "We just need to get something to cut your vest."

"We can't cut his vest!" Miryam said. "That's his Helper Hounds vest. Don't worry. I can get him out."

And with that, Miryam ran back up to the top of the slide and slid down on her stomach toward me.

I yelped and whined.

"I just need to focus," Miryam whispered. Then she breathed deeply. "Focus, focus, focus..."

Miryam told me I was a good boy and that I'd be out soon. She pulled her hair back and put it into a pony tail. "Now my hair won't distract me," she said.

Miryam put one arm around me and her other hand on the part of the vest that got snagged.

"It's just a little loop that got tangled," she yelled out. "I think I can untangle it. Someone count to ten. I can do it!"

Malik stood at the bottom of the slide and starting counting slowly. "One, two, three..."

Miryam grabbed the loop and unwound it. Then she snapped a piece of thread off the vest just as Malik said, "Ten!"

I slid away from the wall of the slide. I was free!

"Got him!" Miryam yelled.

"Okay," Malik said. "Let him go. I'll catch him at the bottom."

Miryam kissed me on the head and moved her arm. I slid to the bottom in no time. I celebrated my freedom by zooming around the yard like crazy.

"That was amazing!" Luke said. "Most people get really nervous in tight spaces. But not you."

"No, once I got my hair out of my face, there was nothing to distract me. It was easy to focus in there! I already got my wiggles out. I gave myself a time limit, *and* I breathed deeply! Now it's time for my reward."

Everyone laughed, but I didn't know what was so funny. It was *definitely* time for a reward. And it was time for Miryam to go back to online learning, especially now that she had new ways to stay focused on her lessons.

EPILOGUE

Dear Brisket:

I just liked that picture you posted of your ripped vest.
Sorry about that! But I'm glad the Helper Hounds
people could fix it for you. I still have a piece of
red thread stuck on that screw. I'll never take it out
because I think of you when I slide past it!

Thanks for introducing me to Zahra. She is amazing. So
funny and smart. Every time we talk online, we laugh
and laugh and laugh. She tells the funniest stories about
some kid named Rufus?

My dad told me if I keep working hard on my
e-learning, he'll take me to London to visit her. At

least, once my immune system gets better, that is. Doctor says maybe next year! Yay!

Maybe you can come too. Luke said you flew over under the seat. That sounds crowded. Maybe that's why you didn't like being stuck in the slide! Ha!

Anyway, talking with Zahra really helps me focus. I've done so much better in school. My teacher liked your tips too. He is working with me on setting time limits. Turns out, I can listen to his boring stories if I know they'll be only a couple minutes long!

Next time Zahra and I talk, you can join us. She says she has another funny story about kale salad? I don't get it. How is kale salad funny? My dad makes me eat it. I think it's okay...

Gotta run. Class is starting!

Love,

Miryam   55

Brisket's
Tips for Focusing (on Online Learning)

Before Class Starts

Create a good space. When Luke started training me, we worked in the main room of our flat. This offered plenty of space and few distractions. When you know you have to do school online, find a comfortable space. It doesn't have to be big, but make sure it has room for your computer, your books, and a notebook. Make sure it's well-lit and keep it free from things that might distract you. So, no phones or games or toys on the desk! However, you can hang your favorite pictures or keep a stuffed friend nearby. If you have a little fidgety toy to squeeze or yoga ball to sit on, that can sometimes help!

Create a road map for the day. It's much harder to focus when you don't know what's coming. So, learn what's coming! Ask your parent or caregiver to help you map out your schedule for the day. List the classes, the website where they're found, and the times they start and finish. Be sure to include breaks.

Get your wiggles out. Luke always took me for a nice long walk before we worked on obedience. This not only helped me get my wiggles out, but also settled me down. The same goes for online learning! A nice morning walk or some time playing outside will help you be able to pay attention longer. Exercise is great for the mind!

During Class

Set a goal by setting your timer. Luke likes to break our training times down into very short sessions—sometimes only a couple of minutes. If you have trouble focusing for a thirty-minute class, try setting a timer for three minutes at first. When you make it to three minutes, celebrate with a sip of your favorite juice or give yourself a gold star. Try to increase the time each day!

Use all your senses. It's hard to stare at a computer all day. So, take a break from looking at the camera and sometimes work on simply listening to the lesson. Tell your teacher this is what you are doing—and take good notes. Otherwise, when you are looking at the screen, try to notice more about the teacher than what he or she is saying. What are his arms doing? What does her face tell you?

Breathe. I don't know why it works, but when I feel nervous or antsy, sticking my tongue out and breathing in and out for a while calms me right down. Luke says the same thing. He does yoga and likes to breathe in (count, one-two-three-four-five) and out (count, one-two-three-four-five). Try it!

Treat yourself! Plan a fun activity or snack at the end of each class—or the end of your day. Luke would give me little treats for my good sits and stays and leave-its, but always offered a really great treat (like a sausage or a playdate at the park with Zahra!) at the end of our full sessions. Talk to your parents or caregiver about some ideas!

FUN FACTS

About Lakeland Terriers

Brisket the Lakeland Terrier is full of energy! That's one of the most important facts about this breed of dog. The Lakeland Terrier has been called "a big dog in a small package. "Lakies" are bold dogs that are fun to be around!

These dogs are named after the Lake District area of northern England. That is where they were first bred. Back in the day, these little dogs had a big job. Farmers kept small packs of these dogs to hunt foxes that killed the farmers' sheep. Lakies were working dogs who performed an important job.

In Great Britain, this dog used to be called by different names. In the past, the breed was called the Elterwater Terrier, Westmoreland Terrier, Patterdale Terrier, Fell Terrier, and Cumberland Terrier. That's a lot of big names for a small dog! Finally, in 1921, this breed got its official name. It's been known as the Lakeland Terrier ever since.

No matter what you call it, a Lakeland Terrier is a little dog with a big attitude. These dogs are curious and like to explore. They have a great sense of smell— which came in handy back in those fox-hunting days--and love to follow their noses in search of something interesting, just like Brisket does in the story.

Lakeland Terriers aren't big. The average male stands just 15 inches high and weighs only about 17 pounds. Females are a little smaller. Its body is narrow, which makes it easy for this dog to squeeze into tight places.

Lakies come in many different colors, including brown, black, and wheat. Sometimes, like Brisket, they have a different-colored marking on their back that looks like a saddle. These dogs have a special "double" coat. The outer layer of fur is stiff and wiry, like a brush. That special fur helps keep the dog dry. The inner layer is soft and helps keep the dog warm.

Lakeland Terriers are high-energy dogs, and the people they live with need to train them and make sure they get lots of walks and playtime. They are curious and love to explore, and sometimes their sense of adventure gets them into trouble! These dogs love people and are happy to spend time with their families. They make wonderful pets—as long as they can "get their zoomies out"!

HELPER HOUNDS

If you loved reading about Brisket, you should discover the other seven Helper Hounds!

Check with your favorite bookstore or library

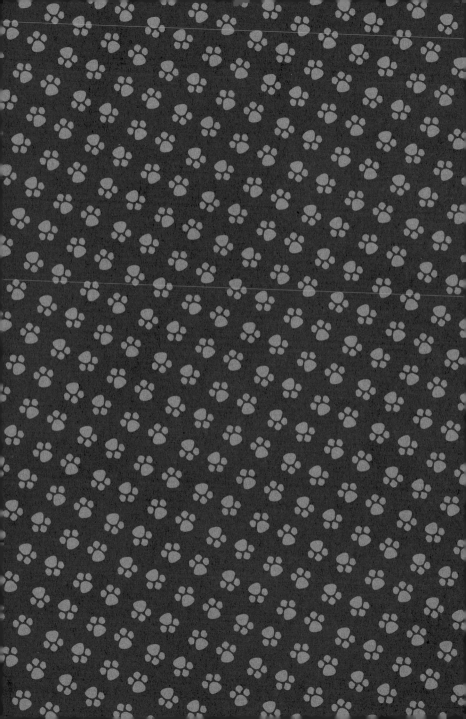